HORACE

AND THE

SECRET RECIPE

Written & Illustrated by DAVID REED

HORACE and the Secret Recipe

Created for 2016 SVA Continuing Education class:
Prof. Monica Wellington
Characters and artwork created using
Apple Ipad Pro & Apple Pencil

-To Mom, Dad, Kim, Talee, and Sarah -

Horace the Slow Loris and Ollie the Owl
are the very best of friends!

Ollie's "secret recipe" is top secret.
Horace helps by going out each day to gather
a new special ingredient for the secret recipe.
Luckily for Horace, he has plenty of forest friends
to help him find the ingredient he needs.

Monday: KALE

Horace has never tried kale before,
but he does know a tiny, slow moving
veggie lover who would be quick to help.

Miss Sadie Snail!

She's so very happy to see Horace
and even happier to help him find
some crisp, green kale.

Tuesday: GRASSHOPPERS

Grass-hoppers?? Horace knows only one kind of hopper. He puts on his yellow boots and heads out to find his muddy swamp buddy. . .

Freddy the Friendly Frog!

The grasshoppers are too fast for
Horace but not for Freddy! He uses
his sticky tongue to catch them one by one.

Wednesday: SWEET POTATO

Horace has eaten a potato before, but one
that is sweet? Who can uncover this mystery?
Grumbles the Groundhog!

Horace is amazed to find out that sweet potatoes grow underground.
Grumbles says regular potatoes hide underground too.
Such clever potatoes!

Thursday: HONEY

Horace loves honey! Its one of his favorite sweet
treats of all, and he knows just where to find it.
He sets off to find his tiny, buzzing buddy. . .

Bitty Bee!

She gives him a teeny, tiny hug, then
brings him some sweet, rich, golden honey.

Friday: PUMPKIN SEEDS

Horace knows if its seeds he needs,
its time to visit his most colorful friend . . .
Tj Toucan!

Tj flies Horace across the sky to a pumpkin
patch with big, bright, orange pumpkins.
Horace decides the most fun way to get seeds is to
squeeze inside of a pumpkin, and inside he goes!

Saturday: **CHERRIES**

Horace loves cherries! He knows exactly
who to visit for a cherry picking adventure . . .
Little Sugar Bear!

One to eat, one in the bag.
One to eat, one in the bag.
The cherry bandits have great fun
picking and gobbling tasty cherries.

Sunday: **THE SECRET RECIPE**

Horace hurries out to see Ollie, already
busy making the secret Sunday recipe.
To his surprise, he also sees Miss Sadie
Snail who helped him find Kale, Friendly
Freddy Frog who caught the hoppers,
Grumbles the Groundhog who dug up
sweet potatoes, itty Bitty Bee with the
sweet honey, Tj Toucan who helped with
pumpkin seeds, and Little Sugar Bear,
the cherry bandit himself!

The secret recipe is delicious.
They eat and laugh and enjoy the
wonderful meal together.

Horace can't help but wonder about
the "secret" for the secret recipe.
Was it magic?
Was it passed down from
Grandfather Owl,
to Poppa Owl,
to Ollie Owl?

"**YOU** are the secret!," Ollie explains.
"You went out to gather all the ingredients
yourself, which always makes food taste better.
You're also eating with all of your friends
who've helped you along the way!"

Horace sits grinning as
Ollie serves dessert:
a slice of cherry pie with sweet honey.

Eating great food surrounded
by those he loves, Horace feels
like the luckiest Slow Loris in
the whole wide world.

THE END

35878902R00017

Made in the USA
Lexington, KY
08 April 2019